CHOSEN ONES

S TEPHEN S LATER

TABLE OF CONTENTS

PROLOGUE

A THOUSAND YEARS AGO an elite group of mercenaries called the Chosen Ones helped a man called Dracell in his last stand for freedom against a formidable foe called the Tragens. Dracell and the Chosen Ones fought alongside one another knowing that their fate would be to stand and fight or to run and die; they chose to fight at the meadow of Umarus. The Tragens were defeated by Dracell with the help of the Chosen Ones and with this defeat the Chosen Ones became the sworn enemies of the Tragens.

In helping Dracell defeat the Tragens, Dracell gave the Chosen Ones a great honour for saving him: he made them the guardians of his life and his lineage that would sit upon the throne created from this great victory. Never again would the Chosen Ones allow the people of this land to be plagued by the Tragens again.

Now peace reigned throughout the Empire for generations, and although it had a few skirmishes at the borders with the Tragens, neither side ever really committed to full-scale war again. That is, until a Tragen spy, masquerading as a captain of the Imperial palace guard, seduced and bedded Frances II's first wife, who eventually gave birth to the spy's son, Clasus. When Clasus became aware of his true fathers identity, he killed the emperor and then betrayed the Chosen Ones by giving their whereabouts to the Tragen army, who purged the Chosen Ones to extinction.

Now that his vengeance on the Chosen Ones was complete, Clasus's bid for the Imperial throne was almost complete, but one thing stood in his way. Two children were born during this turmoil, one was of the Chosen Ones' clan, and the other was Frances's daughter from his second wife. They were hidden and taken into safety by Arthur, the last of the Chosen Ones, before Clasus could get his hands on them.

CHAPTER ONE

THERE WAS A great battle that had happened here in the meadows long ago: that two great army's had stood here ready to fight for honour and freedom. Now it was no more; only shepherds went about the land; they looked after their herds in the meadows of Umarus, completely unaware that this site had forged a great, peaceful Empire a long time ago.

An evil man now sat upon the throne, corrupting and purging the lands for his own benefits – but all that did not concern Sammy, who was a young lad in his mid teens. Sammy lied upon the ground daydreaming of himself as a great warrior in glorious battles yet to come, but he knew that would not happen because he was only a pour shepherd who was trying to make a small living to help support his uncle back in his village.

His village, Viscal, was the furthest northern outpost of the Empire and was in the mountain region, just one mile away from Dracass and one mile west from the famous battleground of Umarus.

It was getting dark now, so Sammy gathered up his herd and was ready to go home when he herd a rider coming his way. He thought it was a thief, so he grabbed his knives, ready to defend himself, Sammy was the best in his village with knives because his uncle had been teaching him how to fight from a young age. Sammy knew that his uncle had been a soldier in his past but didn't know that he was the last of the Chosen Ones, the elite mercenaries that had sworn to protect the Dracell bloodline containing the true heirs to the throne.

Once the rider approached him, Sammy soon realised that it was his best friend, Adria, who had came out to see him and walk back with him to the village. Sammy was very tall for his age; some would say that he was a giant or a troll because with his muscular build of a primed fighter, he towered over any man. All though he looked strong, he was a gentle man who was just a hard worker who did many jobs to help out his village.

Adria was a very beautiful women and was also quit tall herself. Her hair was long and jet black, and she walked around rooms as if she could take command within an instant. As she was getting off her horse to talk to Sammy, Sammy was already approaching her with joy on his face.

"Hello, Adria, what brings you out here?"

"I knew I would find you out here, Sammy; I've come to remind you about tomorrow."

Sammy stood there with a look of confusion on his face thinking about what was supposed to happen tomorrow, but he could not remember.

"I see that you have forgotten again, Sammy. It will be the day when we become adults, you idiot."

"What are you talking about, Adria? Our birthday is not for another week." Sammy knew all too well that they shared the same birthday.

"Sammy, don't you remember that the village always celebrates the coming of adulthood a week before the birthday to show everyone that they have become of age?"

"Of course, I just forget because I have a lot of work to do for the village."

Adria simply smiled at him, and Sammy guess she knew that he had lied to her. "Well, let's make our way back home before it gets any later."

As they walked back to the village, they laughed and joked about the pranks that had done to the village elders. Sammy enjoyed talking about the past until Adria turned around and asked him, "What will become of us when we become adults?"

"What do you mean, Adria? You're not planning to leave the village, are you?"

"No, I'm not leaving Sammy. It is just that Mabel and your uncle are holding secrets from us, and I presume that they will tell us what they are holding back."

"Do you think that these secrets will change our future?"

"I really don't know what will happen to us, Sammy, but I do know this that our friendship will change after tomorrow."

Sammy was puzzled by what she meant, but he said nothing about it and took Adria's hand to comfort her. "Look, Adria, whatever happens tomorrow, we will always be friends. I don't know how anything will change that."

As they walked past the gates of the village, they saw that Mabel, Adria's foster mother, was waiting for them outside the house in her rocking chair. As they reached the house, Sammy took the horse from Adria and led it into the stables to take care of it. Adria waited outside for him, and while she was waiting she noticed that Mabel was looking more pleased then usual. "Why are you so cheerful, Mabel?"

"It's not a crime to smile, is it, Adria?"

"Well no, it is just that you seem happier than usual." Before Mabel could answer that question, Sammy had walked out of the stables.

"Well hello there, Sammy, I did not recognise you. I'm so happy that you are coming of age; I can see that you will become a great man in your life."

"Thank you, Mabel. Well anyway, I think I'd best be off before it gets any later, so good night."

Sammy walked home, and once he entered the house he saw that his uncle was waiting for him by the fire. "Well, don't just stand there, boy, you're letting the cold air in." Sammy closed the door and sat down in a chair that was by a fire. Once Sammy sat down, his uncle turned around and said, "Sammy, we have much to talk about tonight, you and I, and everything that you have known will change." With that he pulled out an amulet from his pocket. "Do you know what this means, Sammy?" he asked, passing the amulet over.

Sammy took the amulet from his uncle and noticed the symbol printed on it: a dragon wrapped around a sword. "This is the symbol of the Chosen Ones," Sammy said, "but I don't understand how you came to have this. That race has been extinct for years."

"They're not extinct, Sammy, although some wish it to be true. I'm the last of the Chosen Ones, Sammy, and that amulet that you are holding now was yours father's. Whoever wore that showed that he was the leader of our clan. Sammy, you are also a Chosen One."

"Is true, then, that the Chosen Ones were betrayed by someone within their own ranks?"

"Yes we were, I'm afraid."

"What happened, Uncle? Why are we now a dying race?"

"A long time ago, we were the guardians of the Dracell blood-line, and until that day is up, we will honour that allegiance."

"Uncle, you have told me about Clasus being a pretender, but how can there be some one of the Dracell bloodline still be alive without you knowing?"

"That's where you are wrong, Sammy. I do know that there is a true heir to throne, and I believe that you know this person, but any-way before we start asking anymore questions, let me tell you what happened. It all began before you were born, with the birth of Clasus from the first wife of Frances II. We knew that it was not a true heir, and we were ordered by the emperor to kill the man that bedded his wife, but he spared Clasus's life, and so we took the child into our ranks and trained him in our methods of fighting. He became a for-midable warrior, but we were foolish to have him in our midst, and I was right about him because once he found out about his true heri-tage, he swore vengeance on us and also the Dracell lineage because he wanted the throne for himself.

"We didn't realise at first that it was Clasus we fought; we were surprised by our enemy overwhelming us with the sheer number of his troops. When the final blow came to us, it was by the Tragen army. They knew exactly where we were hiding, and they complete-ly massacred our people. The only reason I survived was because I was arriving with reinforcements; we managed to push back the Tragen army, but in the end there was nothing we could do. Only three other Chosen Ones survived, including the betrayer: your far-ther and our good friend, Simone, but in the end Clasus had planned his betrayal very well! As we returned to the capital, we found out that the emperor had been poisoned; Clasus blamed it on Malto, the emperor's doctor, and Clasus persuaded the lords of the council to order me to kill Malto, but I no longer trusted Clasus and the people he was friends with, so I decided to disappear with Malto. When I left I took you and Adria into hiding with me to keep you safe."

"Of course!" Sammy said. "How can it not be so obvious: Adria is of the Dracell blood?"

"Yes, and you will be the last of the Chosen Ones when my time is up."

"Don't talk like that, Uncle, you still have a few years left in you."

"No, Sammy, I am afraid it'll soon be my time, and therefore you must go forth and help Adria get her throne back."

"But Uncle, how can I do that all by myself?"

"Once people realise that Adria is alive, they will rally to your cause because they all know that Clasus is a pretender sitting upon the throne. Intriguing, isn't it, boy?"

"Yes," Sammy said cautiously as he took everything in.

"Well, there is more. Come with me, I have something else to show you." Sammy's uncle led him down to the cellar, and there he revealed a secret chamber hidden behind the wine rack. Inside the chamber was brightly lit room with a table in the centre. The table had something on it, but it was covered with a large cloth, and when Sammy entered the chamber he noticed a large sword hanging on a rack on the back wall; it was a magnificent sword that glittered greenish blue in the light. "Well, Sammy, I can see that you have noticed the sword, but that's not all I have to show you," his uncle said, and with that he removed the sheet from the table and revealed other items. "All these things in this room are now yours; they were once mine, but I give them to you. I have no need for them anymore."

"I can't take this, Uncle. I'm no warrior."

"You know, boy, I said those same words to my farther, and you know what he said to me? He said that every man has his own courage in his own way, and he what he does with it will make a warrior in his own right.

"Take the sword, Sammy, and feel the weight of it." Sammy took the long sword of the wall, and once he took it within his hands, the blade of the sword changed colour from the greenish blue to gold. "Well, I can see that sword will be in good hands."

"Why would you say that, Uncle?"

"When I saved Malto's life from Clasus's minions – because I wasn't the only one that was ordered to kill him – with his thanks he blessed that sword with his magic. His magic made the blade invincible, and once he did that he left me a prophecy on that sword. He said that some from my bloodlines will lift that sword, and the blade will turn gold. Once the heir turned it to gold, he would be destined to create a new era with the sword and with his courage from his heart for his lost love."

Sammy was shell shocked from hearing all this from his uncle. "Uncle, how can I take on an Empire for a lost love that I do not have?"

"That's where you are wrong, my boy. Your love could be for anyone you hold dear. For example would you not kill to protect me from harm?"

"I would, Uncle, you know that I would fight for you."

"So you see, my boy, that you are fighting for the love you have for me."

"I think I see your point, Uncle."

"Good, but I think that is all for now. Go get some rest, Sammy. You'll need it; after all, it is your celebration tomorrow." Sammy left for his room to get some sleep with what was left of the night.

CHAPTER TWO

CLASUS SAT ON the Imperial throne, looking down on the play that the jesters were acting in the grand hall for him and his guests. Will he watched the jesters, the captain of the guard appeared before him, and Clasus halted the play so he could hear the captain's report. "My Lord, I've good news for you. I have the wizard Malto that you wanted."

"Excellent. After all these years I finally have him, but what about Arthur, Captain? Did you capture him also?"

"No, My Lord, I am afraid he still eludes me, but with the capture of Malto you maybe be able to persuade him into revealing the whereabouts of Arthur's location."

"Very well, then; bring in your prisoner, Captain." The captain made a signal to his men, and with that two soldiers brought in an old and bruised man into the throne room. "So Malto, you are still alive after all this years?"

"Yes, Clasus, I am still alive, and I know what you want – and you will not have it."

"Oh, don't worry, Malto, I already know were Arthur is," Clasus lied. "All I want to know is where are the children that he took with him."

"How am I supposed to know what he took with him when we went our separate ways, you devil? I should have killed you when you were a child."

"And that, old man, will be your undoing." With that Clasus got up from the dais and walked to Malto, where he whispered into his ear, "Know, Grandfather, this is the end for you, and soon the children that you hid from me will follow you." With these last words, Clasus ended the old man's life by stabbing him in the heart.

All of Clasus's guests were shocked when they saw that he killed this old man in front of them. "My friends, I am sorry for what you have just seen, but he was a traitor of this Empire for killing my father, the late Frances II, and it was in my right to do what he did to my farther. I think we have had enough today, and I think we should all go back to our homes now." With that dismissal his guests and the entertainers left the great hall, and Clasus conferred with his war cabinet. His cabinet members were sitting around a great circular table, and upon the table was a large map of all the neighbouring nations. The map was arranged into different colours for different nations: To the north of the map was red, which represented the Tragen Territories. To the east was a fast ocean with brown and black islands; the brown represented the fast Commonwealth, and the separate black islands belonged to the Empire or the Tragens. The Tragens had only one large island, and the Empire only had two small ones, but only one was populated because everyone believed the other one was cursed. To the south of the map the colour was gold, to represent the desert were the Nomads lived and traded their precious jewels with Empire for water. There was nothing to the west but mountains.

Clasus was more afraid of the Tragens than he was of the children that had been eluding him. The council members were waiting for Clasus, but all he was doing was staring at the map thinking of what needed to be done to keep his throne. "Right, gentlemen, we have a few problems to solve. I want to know where this Arthur is living, and I want to know now."

"My Lord, all we know is that he is somewhere in the mountain region. The problem is that there are six towns and villages and one major city in that area. With the information that you gave us to look for on this person, we would have heard of him; a man in black with two children carrying a long sword would have been noticed by now."

"That was my exact thoughts, General, but I want your spies refreshed on this information again. I want to let them know that it is most important for these people to be found."

"My Lord, sorry for intruding, but does anyone know where this Arthur used to live?"

Clasus turned to the young man, who was new to the council. "Very intriguing. Now why do you ask this?"

"Well, if I was him, My Lord, I would go somewhere that I knew I would be safe, and that would be the place that I had grown up in because I would know the territory well and would be able to trust the people not tell anyone of my whereabouts."

"That is very interesting for you to bring that up because he used to visit Dion, and maybe other places around that area. So that leaves me just two villages around that area, and I think he would go to the furthest village out there."

"That would be Viscal, My Lord."

"Captain Barath, I want you to lead your platoon to this village and capture this man."

"Yes, My Lord. I will go forth now and do what you have commanded."

"Very good. Nothing can stop me now from taking the full succession of this throne."

Chapter Three

It was the day of Sammy's and Adria's celebration of becoming an adult. The two of them stood in front of the village while the elders presented them with gifts that would symbolise them as adults. Adria was given a necklace with an uncut sapphire stone in the centre, and Sammy was given gauntlets that had a bear on them; the bear was standing on his hind legs ready to challenge something.

Once Sammy and Adria were given their gifts, they were presented to the rest of the villagers as adults. All the villagers cheered them for what they had accomplished today, and with that the celebration started. People began to dance to the music, and Sammy and Adria joined them. Arthur and Mabel watched the two with great joy; as the young pair danced together. The old foster parents were happy that Sammy and Adria could find companionship with each other.

Once the first dance had finished, Sammy and Adria joined Arthur and Mabel at the table. "Well you two seem pleased, but it is not over just yet," Mabel said, and with that she pulled out a cloth and unravelled it on the table to reveal two rings. "These rings are for you two." To Adria she passed a silver ring with a copper stone, and upon the stone was a symbol of a horse's head, which was the symbol of the Dracell family. "See, Adria, what I told you last night was true."

"I couldn't believe it until now that I am the true heir to the Dracell Empire and that Sammy is a Chosen One that has sworn to protect me."

"Indeed, my dear. And Sammy, this ring is for you." Mabel passed him a plain silver ring with some engraving of the Chosen Ones' motto: "Courage is our soul."

Arthur put his hand on Sammy's shoulder and said, "Well done, my lad, you have fully become a man and maybe a warrior. Oh don't just stand there; the pair of you go on back to celebration. It's all yours, after all."

As the two of them rejoined the dancing and were congratulated by others, a lone rider came striding into the village. The stranger was dressed in all black with a hood to covering the face, and when the rider got of the horse one could clearly see a quiver of arrows and a longbow. This mysterious stranger approached Arthur with the horse in tow. Arthur didn't turn around when the stranger approached him, but he said, "Hello, Madia, it's been a long time, hasn't it my dear?"

"Yes, Father, it has," Madia said as she removed the hood.

Arthur finally turned to look at her and said, "I see a beautiful woman has come out of the young girl that I found on streets all those years ago."

"Father, I have come here with great urgency to tell you something that could cost you your life."

"Yes, I was wondering why my master spy would come all the way out here."

"Father, please listen. Clasus has found out where you are and has sent a platoon of soldiers to get you."

"Madia, don't give me look of pity; I don't want it. I know what you going say, and no, I will not flee, because this is my home and I'm going to stay here and meet my fate as a Chosen One."

"Father, you will die!"

"Yes, no doubt I will, but I will meet it with a blade. Nevertheless, there is one thing you can do for me."

"What is it?"

"I want you take Sammy and Adria to the city of Ferlinzer and seek out a Nomad called Shakall. He will help you out with what needs to be done with those two."

"I will do this, Farther, I promise this to you."

"I have no doubt that you will keep your word to me, my dear, but you must help your brother, for he will need it for when the time comes."

***

Captain Barath had two more days of travel to get to the village of Viscall. Barath had to make camp that day because he had just made an exhausting march to get where he was now. Barath knew he needs to make up the time to get where Arthur was, so he had pushed the horses to the limit and near exhaustion. Once the fire was created for warmth, Barath sat by it to warm himself, and there he contemplated the man he was sent out to capture. Barath new nothing about this man called Arthur; he knew that he was a Chosen One, the legendary warriors, but all this Chosen One nonsense was a myth, a legend passed down by fathers through stories. Barath and his brother loved to hear the stories that his father would tell them about the Chosen Ones. Now he was ordered to capture this man, and it was the only way to be moved up in rank and privilege. He really did want his rewards for the capture, but he did not wish any harm to be brought upon the villagers.

***

It was a strange day for Sammy because his uncle was acting very peculiar after the celebration. Although Sammy was leaving that day, he couldn't bear to see his uncle like this. "Uncle, what troubles you so much? Is it because I am leaving today?"

"No, my boy, it is not – and I see that you are wearing my old uniform; it fits you perfectly. Come, boy, I believe the girls are waiting for you outside."

"What about you, Uncle?"

"Don't worry about me; my time is almost at an end, but yours has only just begun. Live it well, my boy. Now, go before it is too late."

With Arthur's words in his mind, Sammy left his house and joined Adria and Madia. He took one final look at his house before he mounted his horse. "You know, Adria, I am going to miss this place."

"So am I, Sammy. I'm even going to miss your uncle, too!"

"Yes, me too. I'm afraid that it will be the last time I am ever going to see him alive. Come on, you two, it is about time that we got a move on," Sammy said, trying to sound more grown-up than he felt. The three of them began to travel down the south passage with the quest of redemption and adventure that Sammy had always dreamed of.

***

At the same time the trio was leaving Viscal via the south, Captain Barath entered into the village throw the northern pass. His men entered at a slow pace because there was no one about to be seen – until they entered the main square, and there standing alone was an old man holding a short sword and looking directly straight at them. "That is far as you go, Captain!"

"Out of my way, old man. I've come here to arrest the traitor called Arthur, captain of the Chosen Ones."

"You have found him. I am the man that you looking for."

"Arthur, you are under arrest for treason against the Empire."

"Then come and get me, Captain, because I will not go without a fight."

"Very well, you shall have your wish. Corporal, take five men and arrest that man."

The Corporal moved off with his men to arrest Arthur, who gave Captain Barath a salute with his sword by raising it to his head, and with that signal an archer appeared on a nearby hill and fired arrows upon Barath's company, killing many men. Arthur gave another signal, and the firing stopped.

"What do you really want, traitor?" bellowed Captain Barath.

"What I want, Captain, is to make sure that you will leave these villagers alone after we are done here!"

"That was my intention to begin with. I only came here for you, no one else."

"Then I have you word, Captain, that no one else will come to harm?"

"You have my word, old man, that none of the villagers will be punished."

"Very well, then. Let us fight just between us." With that Arthur moved into a fighting stance, ready to take on Barath's men and they came at him. Arthur was ready for them; he danced around the soldiers with great ease, and it was an amazing for everyone to see. It was like Arthur was fighting in his prime again. Every time Barath would send more men, in Arthur would cut them down without hesitation, but eventually his age caught up with him because his pace and movements started to slow down. Only his experience kept him alive for the next few minutes, but in the end that was not enough; a soldier took a lucky swing at Arthur and caught him across the chest. But Arthur would not give up; like a dying tiger, he was more dangerous at the end. Knowing his death was near, he wouldn't allow anyone near him, still swinging his sword at anyone that would come close.

Once Barath saw that Arthur had gone down, he approached Arthur and managed to take Arthur's sword away from him. "Easy, old man, it is done now. You have won; none of the villagers shall be harmed, so rest knowing that and go in peace." With that Arthur smiled at his victory and then died for what he wished for: with a sword in his hand as a true warrior.

When Barath eventually let go of Arthur's body, he looked up and noticed an old woman standing above him and holding a long, black sheet. "Don't worry, Captain, we will bury your men for you."

At this comment Barath became fully aware of the six men he had left – from the thirty-man platoon that he had originally started with. "Thank you," he managed to choke out.

"You're welcome. You know, Arthur was a good man and a good friend to most of us," The woman said with a bit of accusation in her voice.

"I am really sorry for what I had to do, but I must take his body to Clasus."

"Yes I know that. Here, wrap this around his body." with that he took Arthur's body and what was left of his men to Rabien, the capital of the Empire.

CHAPTER FOUR

T WAS TWO days later when Sammy and his companions reached Ferlinzer. "What are we supposed to do, Madia, now that we have reached Ferlinzer?" he asked.

"We are supposed to find a man called Shakall, who is a Nomad trader working in this area."

"Do you know what he looks like?"

"No, I am afraid I don't know much about this person," Madia admitted.

"How about asking one of the village people?" asked Adria. Upon hearing this comment the others started to laugh. Adria looked very angry for what they were doing and said, "Well, aren't you going tell me what is so funny?"

"Oh don't worry, Adria, we are not laughing at you. What you just said was funny because we may be able to ask them, but we will get nothing out of them because they do not trust us and will never betray their own," Madia explained.

"Why would they not trust us?" asked Adria.

"Well, we can blame Clasus for that; his greed has made the Nomads not trust anyone anymore. He has forced the Nomads to give up their precious stones for the water that they need to live."

"Come, Adria, it's getting late, and we need to find some place to stay for the night," Sammy said.

The three of them carried on down the street until they found the nearest inn called the Looters Inn. A small man approached them once they came near. "Hello, ladies and sir. Do you wish to stay at my humble inn?"

"Yes we would like to stay here for the night," Madia replied.

"Welcome then, please come in." At the owner's greeting, two young boys came out and took the group's horses and led them to a barn in the back to be taken care of.

Once the travellers entered the inn, they were shown to a table while they waited for their rooms to be ready. As they sat down they started to look around to see whether they could pick out this man called Shakall. "Well, Madia, how are we supposed to find out who this Shakall looks like?" Sammy asked.

"I don't know. In the end we might have to resort to asking around to find out about him."

"There will be no need to do that!" said a voice from behind them, and they all turned around to see a middle-aged man sitting at a nearby table and dressed in the Nomad's orange garments. When they took a closer look at him, they noticed that he had been in many battles; a scar went across his right eye that was clearly from a sword. "Well, you heard me, there's no need to ask anyone about him, because I am Shakall." Shakall got up and joined them at their table. "Oh, don't worry, I know who you three are. But you, lad," he said, pointing at Sammy, "I thought you were my old friend Arthur, but with that Nomad look about you, I know now that you must be his nephew, Sammy!"

"Hang on there, what are you talking about? Sammy isn't a Nomad." said Adria.

"Yes he is, my dear. He has the blood of a Nomad running through his veins."

"I don't understand," Sammy said, quite confused.

"It's quite simple really: Sammy's mother was Nomad, and she was my daughter."

"That explains it a lot then," Madia said. "Sammy, take a look at Shakall's jacket: it has the same bear symbol that you have on your gauntlets."

"I see you have sharp eyes, Shakall replied. "Yes, the bear is the symbol of my clan, and I gave those gauntlets to your elders to give to Sammy when he was older. Well, I think we have had enough of digging into the past. Let's get to the point of why you three are here seeking me out?"

"My father asked me to seek you out and ask you to help with these two," Madia said.

"Really, and why would you need my help?"

"Well, Shakall, what would you say if I told you the true heir to Dracell line is alive?"

"Impossible; that child died years ago without a chance."

At that comment Adria extended her hand in front of her and showed her ring. "I'm that child, and I am still alive thanks to Arthur."

"That sly old dog!" Shakall said with a barking laugh. "So he did do it, taking you two into hiding right under Clasus's nose." Shakall was slapping his legs, clearly amused at what his friend had done.

Sammy became nervous at the glances they were receiving from the other patrons. "Do you think it is wise that we talk about this out in the open?" he asked.

"Of course you're right, Sammy. Have you got anywhere private to talk?" Shakall said.

"Well, I think the only place private would be our rooms."

The four entered one of the rooms given to them. They all grabbed a chair and took it to the fire, which was burning strongly and giving off a comfortable heat. Before Shakall sat down with the others, he noticed Arthur's long sword leaning against the wall by the fire. "I see that Arthur had given you his sword?"

"Yes he has given me everything that was once his," Sammy said.

"Good to see that. By any chance, did the blade turn to gold when you held it, because if it did then the prophecy is true then."

"What prophecy?"

"Well this prophecy began before your Empire was formed; a strange man came to us on a pilgrimage seeking out a Nomad warrior with a Chosen One background. We were confused by this because we had not had any connection with outsiders before. So the rarest thing happened: all the tribes got together to speak to this man. Never before had we done that, considering the feuds we had between each other. While we gathered to hear this man, he told all of us that he was seeking out a man half Nomad and half Chosen One carrying a long sword that had a golden blade. We did not know what he was talking about and told him so. Once he heard this, he realised that he had made a mistake and he was talking about the future. This mysterious man apologised to us and left us a prophecy: that one day that a man of mixed blood would come and seek us out for help, and with him he would have the heir to the Dracell line – and when we did decide to help this mixed-blood man, he would unite the tribes like never before."

"Hang on a minute," Sammy said, "this prophecy is wrong. How can I unite the tribes when they have had feuds between each other for centuries? They will never unite because of this."

"Don't worry about that, Sammy. Since the mysterious man came all those years ago, the tribes have stopped fighting one another over petty things; although we don't always get along with each other, we get together and talk about our differences now."

"Well, thank you for being confident that I can do this, Shakall, and if I can do this, does that mean that you will help us?"

"Yes, I will – and we need to move quickly because the longer the two of you stay together, the greater the danger you are in."

"What are you talking about, Shakall? We are in no danger." Sammy said

"That's where you are wrong. Clasus has had sent his spies out looking for you two, so while you two are together you are in danger. What we need to do is split you two up; it will be the only way to keep you safe from Clasus until we are ready to strike back."

"Where will we go?" Adria asked.

"Well, that's easy enough: Sammy will come with me to the desert, and Madia, you'll have to take Adria to Dione and seek out the physician Lato there. Do you know the town?" Madia nodded. "Good, then we will go our separate ways tomorrow morning – oh, and one more thing: when you see Lato, speak these words to him, and he will know that he has to help you. 'Farek dak teem.' It means, 'The legend is born.'")

Adria looked saddened by what she was hearing. She obviously did not want this to happen; Sammy and Adria had never been separated before. He reached over, grabbed Adria's hand, and said, "What's wrong, Adria?" Madia and Shakall had noticed this dilemma, and apparently they decided to leave the two alone for the night;

they departed quietly. Once Sammy saw the others walk out of the room, he spoke more openly to Adria. "Come on, Adria, tell me what's really going on. Why are you upset?"

"I am afraid, Sammy," she replied.

"I don't understand. What could you possibly be afraid of?"

"I'm afraid for us, Sammy; we have never been separated like this before."

"I know it will be hard for us, but we will always be friends no matter what." Sammy was just about to get up and leave when Adria grabbed his arm.

"Don't leave, Sammy. I don't want to be left alone tonight."

"Don't worry, Adria, there is nothing to be afraid of. I will always be here for you." Sammy kissed Adria on the forehead, and at this Adria moved her head up so she could kiss him on the lips. Through the passion of her kiss, Sammy knew she did love him with all her heart.

After the kiss they both got up and embraced each other. As they kissed each other again, Sammy removed Adria's shirt, showing her firm breasts to him. They moved to the bed, taking more clothes off, and they embraced each other and their love for one another. With that night everything that they had with each other changed.

***

During that night after their passionate love, Adria had a weird dream about Sammy. He was dressed in Nomad garments and was fighting Clasus with an unknown technique that she had never seen before. Her dream took her around the room that she knew as the great hall of the Imperial palace, and there she saw Mabel and Madia holding identical twin babies in their arms, but like mist her dream quickly vanished, and she woke up with sweat running down her face. She did not know what think about the dream; was it so real to her because it was a vision, or was it just her conscience showing her fears to her through a dream? Adria couldn't get back to sleep because of the dream, and with the sun coming up she decided to get out of bed.

***

In the morning Sammy woke up, and when he tried to put his arm around Adria on the other side of the bed he realised she was not there. He shot up to find out if she had left, but she hadn't; she was sitting in a chair cooking breakfast for the both of them. Adria turned around and smiled at Sammy. "Good morning. Are you hungry?"

"Yes!" Sammy got out of bed and washed himself, and then he joined Adria for breakfast, savouring their moments with each other.

CHAPTER FIVE

CAPTAIN BARATH EVENTUALLY made it back to the Imperial palace after his disastrous mission at Viscal, and he tried to hold his head high. Barath entered the great hall with what was left of his men; they were carrying Arthur's body still wrapped up in the black sheet. "My Lord, I bring good news for you: I have the body of Captain Arthur, the last Chosen One."

"Well done, Captain, you have done well. Tell me, were there any young adults with him?"

"No, sir, I didn't see any."

"Very well then. Captain, for your success I promote you to Major. Now leave me and report to General Naider once you have finished disposing of that traitor."

After Barath had left the grand hall, Clasus collapsed back down onto the throne. Clasus hated Arthur so much that he wished that he had killed the old man himself, but the one thing that he so desperately wanted was the children that Arthur hid from him all those years ago. Clasus knew now that he needed to redouble his efforts, so he called in his master spy, General Mardok, to tell his spy network to look for a young man with a long sword; now that boy was the key to his complete control of the Empire.

***

While Clasus was setting things into motion, Madia had just arrived at Dione with Adria. Madia had to find Lato's house, and soon, because Adria needed rest. She had not been feeling very well on their journey and had been sick most of the time. They were just making their way down a street towards the doctor's house when Madia noticed a sign on a derelict house:"*Logs for sale, wet or dry.* "Well I'll be dammed. Shakall was right after all," Madia said.

"Did you not believe him?"

"No I didn't, Adria; how can I? I am a spy, after all, and that sign that I just saw was a message for me, telling me what Shakall told us is true: he is looking for you and Sammy."

The two of them stopped talking to each other and continued down the road they were already on until they reached a white house that was at the bottom of the road. "We're here, Adria, this is the house that we want." Madia helped Adria off her horse and then led her to the front door. Once they reached the door, an old man answered. "How can I help you fine couple today?" Madia just realised that she was hiding her appearance to him; it was a habit that she had as a spy, and she didn't let her guard down so she could help her friend. "Forgive us, Lato, but a friend of yours sent us out here to you, and he says, 'Farak dak teem.'"

Lato raised an eyebrow, clearly intrigued. "I think you two better come in, then. Oh, don't worry about your horses; my apprentice, Kit, will take care of them."

Lato led the two of them into the living room. "Please make yourself at home while I'll go and make some tea for you two." Once Madia and Adria were seated in the two most comfortable chairs provided for them, Lato came back in with refreshments. After he had served them the tea, he sat down next to them. "Now tell me, what kind of trouble has Shakall put me in for helping you two out?"

Madia removed her hood before she spoke to him. "Hopefully not much. We need for you to hide her from Clasus for us."

"And why is she so important to Clasus?"

"She is the true heir to the Dracell throne, and Shakall has gone back to the desert with my brother to gain support from your people."

"Well then, Elmak, I will do what I can." Madia's eyes widened when he mentioned her code name, meaning "shadow." Lato noticed her shock and said, "Oh don't worry, my dear, we have known who you are for quite some time now." Madia suddenly realised that she and Clasus weren't the only ones with spies.

Adria interrupted the conversation. "Excuse me, but I am not feeling too well, Where is your bathroom, please?"

"It's just down the corridor my dear."

After Adria left for the bathroom, Madia looked back at Lato and said, "She has been like that for the past few days now."

"I wouldn't worry about it; it will pass soon enough."

"I don't understand."

"She has morning sickness."

"How! Oh never mind, I know who the farther is, and we mustn't tell him; his enemies will use that against him."

"She might want him to know that she is carrying his child."

"Don't worry, I will talk to her and let her know that she will be in more danger now that she is pregnant."

"I will keep her safe here for as long as possible, but I don't know about you."

"I cannot stay here; I must leave tomorrow for Viscal and find out what happened about my father and Adria's foster mother."

"Madia, I'm afraid that I 'm a bearer of bad news about your father: he died not long after you had left, but be glad to know that he died as warrior, with honour." Adria had just walked in on the conversation and looked shocked that Arthur was dead.

"Adria why didn't you tell me that you are pregnant?" Madia asked her.

"How did you know?"

"It was Lato that spotted the symptoms. Why, Adria?"

"I didn't know myself until this morning; I need to tell Sammy that he's going to be a father."

"You can't, Adria!"

"Why not? He has the right to know!"

"Listen to me, of course he has the right, but we can't tell him now; he will be in more danger if you do – and so will you. Clasus fears you both, so think what he will do if he found out if you are with child He will use you to get to Sammy and kill you before your child is born."

At that point a young boy came in the room, and Lato said, "Ah, they you are, Kit. Ladies, this is my apprentice; he will be showing you to your room, Adria." Adria followed Kit to the room and could clearly see that it was bigger then she had expected, but she didn't really care; all she wanted to do was go to sleep.

After a good night's sleep, Adria was feeling a bit better and could eat something properly, so she decided to go downstairs and have breakfast. There she saw Madia readying to leave for Viscal. Once they said their good-byes, Adria watched Madia ride off to Viscal. Adria held her stomach thinking of the family that would be hers once this child was born – but at what cost?

CHAPTER SIX

SAMMY AND SHAKALL finally arrived at the Nomad border after three days' travailing. They were both tired and in need of rest. At the border outpost, there wasn't much to show but a couple of mud huts and a large cattle pen that was holding a couple of camels inside. "Lad, we will stay here for the night."

"I do have a name you know, Shakall."

"Do you really? Well, that will be remedied soon enough; we'll find you a better one that will suit you. Now come, a storm is approaching, and we'd better get inside before it gets here."

Sammy followed Shakall into the hut, where there were other Nomads waiting out the storm. As soon as he closed the door behind him, the other Nomads started speaking in their own language: "Farak dak teem." ("The legend is born.") "Dacass tak too." ("Golden-blade slayer.") But what they did not realise was that Sammy could clearly understand them; it was natural for him to understand them, and now he knew that he was part Nomad he knew why he could easily understand their language.

It had only been a few hours when the storm had finally passed. Shakall grabbed Sammy's shoulder. "Come, lad, it is time that we leave here and head for my settlement." They both left the hut and headed towards the cattle pen, but instead of the horses that they brought with them Shakall got hold of two camels.

"Camels, what's wrong of our horses?" asked Sammy.

"We are using these instead of our horses because they will take us further while using less water." With that Shakall got on his camel, and Sammy copied him. "Good lad. It seems that I will make a Nomad out of you after all."

"I don't think that I will have a choice in this, will I?"

"Oh but you will, my lad. But if you wish to survive, you must learn to understand people's customs; it is the only way to gain their respect."

Sammy and Shakall seemed to come to an understanding with each other, and they set of into the desert. Before they went into full gallop, Shakall passed Sammy a sheahmag so he could cover up his face to protect from the dust as they rode through the dessert. Shakall was amused that Sammy was able to put it on without any help; it seemed that Sammy was getting more acquainted with the Nomads' ways as they travelled through the desert together. As Sammy finished putting it on, he looked at Shakall and said, "Now where?"

"We shall head west to an oasis; that's where my settlement will be."

***

On that same day Clasus was pleased for once because he had just received some good new at last, but the news did not contain information about the children that he wanted; it was about the Tragens. His spies had told him that Osesus, the Tragen's leader, had just died without leaving an heir to succeed him, and fighting had broken out between different families to see who had the right of succession. With the Tragens at civil war, they couldn't be a threat to Clasus anymore – only the children that still eluded him could haunt his dreams now. Then all of a sudden Clasus remembered something about one of these children. "General Mardok?" Mardok appeared out of the shadows. "I want you to send fresh information to your spies that one of these children that they are looking for would be a fully grown lady with jet black hair. She will be very tall for her age; that will be the one I want the most."

***

Sammy and Shakall had finally reached the oasis, and as Sammy looked around he could clearly see many tents and animals in the area. As he got closer he noticed that the Nomads were armed with swords and spears. The armed guards saluted their clan leader as Shakall passed them, but when the armed guards noticed Sammy still dressed in the clothes that his uncle gave him, they said, "Fagarath" (outlander). They started calling him this curse that they have given everyone that wasn't a Nomad; they also spat at him because they disliked outlanders due to the treatment that they had been given from Clasus. "You see now, lad, why we hate outlanders so much, because Clasus has cheated us out of the water we need."

As they reached where they needed to go, one of the soldiers that was escorting them spotted Sammy's sword strapped across his back. The soldier's eyes were wide with shock and delight when he saw this sword, so he decided to run through the camp screaming,"Farak dak teem" as loud as he could. All the Nomad members started to appear to see what all the commotion was all about, and when they saw this strange man riding with their leader towards his tent, they remembered thelegend that they. where told as children

Two young boys came out of the large tent to collect the camels from Sammy and Shakall. Sammy entered the tent and saw a middle-aged woman standing in the middle. "Hello, Shakall, welcome back. I hope your journey went well?"

"It did, my dear. Lad, this is my wife, Tasmea."

"Doesn't he have a name, Shakall?"

"Yes, but not a good one, my love. I believe he will need a Nomad name."

"Hello, I am still here, you know. And I always liked the name Danrak," Sammy said. The name he had chosen meant chameleon.

"So sorry about that, lad. Yes, I do believe that name will suit you well. Danrak it is."

Tasmea looked at Sammy's clothes and clearly did not like what she saw. "Those garments will not do here, I'm afraid. You will need proper clothing if you're going to become a Nomad." She summoned a young servant boy, and as the young boy entered the tent he was already carrying clothes for Sammy. Tasmea took the clothes from the boy and passed them over to Sammy. "Here you go, Danrak, this will fit you nicely. Go on, put them on." Sammy changed into the Nomad clothes; the only thing that he kept on was the medallion and the ring that was given to him to show that he was still a Chosen One and among his people.

Shakall grabbed Sammy once he was done getting dressed. "Come, Danrak, it is time to learn our ways before we can even think of talking before the council." Sammy followed Shakall outside the tent towards an open area, in the middle of which was a circular rope that was ankle high.

Sammy was puzzled by this because he had never seen anything like it before. "What is this for, Shakall?"

"This ring is called caca da ran (warriors circle), and this is where you will begin your training as a warrior."

"I don't need any training because I am already a warrior."

"Really? Okay, then, if you believe you are a fully trained warrior, how about you show me what you can do in a little contest against one of our half-trained warriors?"

"Okay, I will, but I think it is a bit unfair for that young man."

"We shall see, won't we." Sammy didn't like that Shakall said this with an evil grin upon his face.

"I think I'm beginning to have second thoughts about this, but I will meet him with an open mind."

"That is all I ask of you, Danrak"

"Where is this person that I am supposed to fight?"

"He is over there," Shakall said, pointing to a small young man with an athletic build.

Sammy smiled once he saw his opponent because he could clearly see that he had a clear advantage over him with his height and build, but he would always remember the one thing that his uncle had taught him: to never underestimate your enemy because appearances could be deceiving. Sammy entered the ring to face his opponent, and once the chime rang, the fighting commenced. Sammy went into the attack first, throwing different combinations of punches into his opponent just to test defences, but the man just stood there and took it as they were nothing but just a slap to him. Sammy finally caught him with a left uppercut and knocked the man on his back, and he thought that he had won the fight, but he hadn't.

The man did something so unexpected that it caught Sammy off guard: the man did a back flip to bring himself back up on his feet, and he came back at him with kicks and punches. Sammy was lucky enough that he was able to hold him off for a while, but in the end it was too much for him; the onslaught overpowered his defences, and the man changed his style of fighting by using his open palms, knees, and elbows. Sammy didn't know how to defend against this, and then the man swept out Sammy's legs from underneath him and brought his elbow into his chest, which knocked the wind out of him. Once Sammy was down on his back and could not get back up with the wind knocked out of him, the chime sounded to end the fight between them two.

After the fight Sammy's opponent helped him back up to his feet. "Thank you for that lesson," Sammy said. "I didn't get your name, by the way."

"It is Takar, and I am honoured that you fought against me."

"I am honoured also, Takar, and I believe that we shall learn much from each other."

There was a sound of applause from Shakall when they shook hands in gratitude. "Well done, you two. I believe you will do well together. Danrak, what do you think– are you already a warrior?"

"I see your point now, Shakall. Will you teach me, then?"

"That was my whole idea from the beginning, but you didn't listen; arrogant men never listen. It was your pride that became your downfall, Danrak."

"My pride? But my uncle taught me to never underestimate my enemy."

"Your uncle was a wise man and a great warrior, even against us, because he knew how to let go of his pride, and that is why he was a formidable warrior. In time you will learn to let go as well, and perhaps you will be better than even your uncle. Come, let's go and get your wounds looked at. Tomorrow we shall begin your proper training."

"And then let's hope that my pride shall go before a fall."

"Well said, Danrak; you are beginning to learn already."

"Thank you." Sammy then turned to Takar. "My friend, I will see you tomorrow for training." With that the two fighters departed to different tents. Sammy entered his tent and collapsed on some cushions, tired from his ordeal, but soon enough he remembered

Adria and Madia, and he was wondering what they were up to. He was thinking that Adria was right about one thing: their friendship did change after they left their village, and now he felt saddened that he was thinking of them because he missed her and wanted to be near her and hold her. However, Sammy he knew that could not happen because they would be in great danger if he went to her.

***

After some rest Sammy finally awoke the next day, and standing above him was Takar. "Good morning, did you sleep well? Because if you didn't, you will tonight, I guarantee it." With that Sammy joined Takar outside for their training.

Once they reached the ring again, Shakall was already waiting for them. "Oh good, there you are. We have much work ahead of us today. Let us begin." Shakall passed them both a staff. They took the staffs and started to attack and defend against each until they were both nearly exhausted. "Good, very good, but lets try this, shall we?" Shakall said as he blindfolded Sammy. "Now Danrak, I want you to learn how to use your other senses instead of your eyes. Takar is going to attack you, and you must listen out for him and anticipate his movements." Before Sammy could understand what was going on, Takar already struck him with his staff. Sammy did not like that he could not use his eyes in this test, and in the end he had to use his ears and other senses that he now just started to become aware of; he could feel where Takar was, and with that he blocked everything that came his way. It was as if he had a shield around him because nothing was getting through his defences. Shakall was pleased by what he saw from Sammy and his unstoppable aura, so he stopped the test and dismissed them for the day.

***

Sammy's training progressed quickly during the next two months, and Takar was doing well, too. In fact they were both doing so much better than expected that soon Shakall decided to put them in the final test to become a Nomad warrior. "You two will be going in for your final test today. You must defeat a fully trained warrior, and I am afraid that you are first, Danrak, to go into the ring."

Sammy stepped into the ring and faced his opponent and again he waited for the chime. This time when the chime rang, Sammy didn't charge out; he just stood his ground. It was his opponent that came charging at him, but before the man could reach to do anything, Sammy threw two side kicks at him, and before his second kick was over he brought his body into full roundhouse kick, knocking the man across the ring, unconscious. Shakall was shocked that the fight ended so quickly, and he barely managed to find his voice when Sammy approached him. "Well done. Danrak, I am speechless/ I don't know what to say; that was amazing, I never expected to see that from anyone."

"Shakall I've said it before and I will say it again: never underestimate your enemy."

"Yes indeed, it looks as if I am going to learn things from you. Now it is Takar's turn. Let's go and see how he gets on, shall we?"

Sammy and Shakall rejoined the ring and watched Takar's test. Sammy recognised Takar's opponent: it was the guard that ran past him the day he arrived at the settlement. The chime rang again to begin their fight; both men came at each other within the middle of the ring with aggressive intent to win, throwing punches at one another and trying to get that winning strike. Takar was struggling because the other man was a bit too quick for him to handle, but when he saw his opening to gain victory, he took it by throwing the same uppercut that Sammy had hit him with, knocking the man flat on the floor, and with this blow Takar had won his fight.

Shakall congratulated Takar on his success. "Well done to the both of you, and it with the greatest honour as the leader of this clan that I now make you Nomad warriors."

Sammy and Takar congratulated each other. "Well, Takar, I am in need of a good warrior and a good friend."

"Then you have both, because we are now brothers." Takar said with a smile.

"Good because I will need your help when I talk to the tribe leaders in two weeks' time."

"I will help you create the army you are going to need – and it will be a formidable army, indeed."

CHAPTER SEVEN

MADIA HAD FINALLY made it back to her village, Viscal. It was hard and long for her because she had to make a few stops along the way to gain information about what had happened since she had gone. As Madia entered the village, she noticed that there were fresh graves within the village cemetery, and she was saddened that many people had to die just for them to escape Clasus's clutches. Madia needed answers for what happened at the village, so she decided to find Mabel and hoped she would tell her what she needed to know – and she also needed to tell her about Adria.

Madia reached Mabel's house to speak to her, but Mabel had already noticed her. "Hello, Madia, nice to see you back. How are Sammy and Adria?"

"They were both fine when I left them, and I have some good news about those two also, but I believe it not wise talk about them two out here in the open."

"I think we'd better get inside, then, and make ourselves comfortable if we are going to have much to talk about." Madia followed Mabel into her kitchen and sat down in one of the chairs. Mabel joined her with some tea for them both. "Well go on, now, tell me what burdens you, Madia?"

"Mabel, I have come back to find out to what really happened to my father."

"Well, not long after you three left, a platoon of soldiers arrived to arrest your father, but we attacked them to gain time for your escape. Many people died, but the captain who was in charge was an honourable man; he didn't want any innocent blood taken that day, so he agreed to a deal with your father that his men would only fight him in a duel. Your farther fought gallantry, Madia, but he was too old to beat them all. He took a deadly wound when he was fighting the soldiers and died fighting to the bitter end. I miss the old fool; he was a very good friend to me over the years." Both women had to wipe their eyes for a few moments before Mable spoke again. "But let us forget our sorrows, Madia, and talk about Adria and Sammy."

"As you wish. Sammy is down south with the Nomads organising an army for our cause."

"What! Nomads? How can they go up Clasus's elite shock troopers?"

"I don't know, but with Sammy now involved with the Nomads, anything is possible."

"Yes, I wouldn't doubt that the boy could do anything if he put his mind to it. And what about Adria, where is she?"

"She is with a newfound friend, Mabel. And I am afraid she is pregnant. She has at least a few weeks left before she goes into labour, I think. I must be going back soon."

"Then I am going with you, Madia. I want to see my foster daughter and my future grandchild."

"Very well, then we will leave in the morning, so get some rest because we have some hard travelling ahead of us." Madia got up to leave.

"Where are you going Madia?"

"Home!"

"You could stay here, you know."

"I know, but I wish to be alone tonight."

Madia left for her own house that she had grown up in. The house was as she had remembered during her childhood years; even her old room that her father had kept for her was the same.

It was early in the morning when Madia awoke to begin her journey back to Dione. Mabel was already waiting outside for her with the horses, and they started their journey. "Wear to then, Madia?"

"We must go south and find a old friend of mine; it will be at least eighteen days of travel before we will get there, and then we will go to Adria, that I promise you."

***

By now Clasus was growing impatient that he wasn't getting anywhere with these young adults that he was after. Clasus was getting so much erratic information about three companions. Two people might have fit the description of the people that he wanted, but when they tried to get more information on them, they vanished without a trace. It was all up to General Mardok now to gain more information, and his plan was to seek out this third person that was their guide and helped them – and therefore would know where they went into hiding. Clasus was certain that for the right price, the guide would reveal that information to him.

CHAPTER EIGHT

THE NEWLY PROMOTED Major Barath was now assigned as an intelligence officer to General Naider, the supreme commander of the Imperial forces. His new job was a tiring one: he had to gain information from internal and external threat against Clasus. Barath was an honourable man that hated Clasus and wished for a better person to be upon the throne, but there was no one else to replace him. He only wished there was an alternative, but until he found a way to overthrow Clasus he would obey Clasus's orders to a certain extent because enough of innocent lives had been lost in the name of Clasus's jealousy and greed for total control.

While Barath was going through some reports, he believed that he found a way out of his dilemma because in one of the reports he had found a mysterious person called Elmak. When he began to take a close look at the reports, they clearly showed some more information about this person. Although some of the information that he came across was too farfetched to believe, he managed to get some information on Elmak that was reliable, but in the end he had to make an educated guess on what was true and false on this person. If ever Barath wanted to get out now, he needed to seek out this Elmak – but how would he find him! This man was a phantom, and trying to find him wouldn't be easy. With Barath still in his thoughts he didn't notice one of Mardok's aids until the man put another report on his desk. The report was just the usual things that Barath had already read, but then he came across the bottom of the report: a man called Danrak had called a council meeting among the Nomad tribes. Barath found this very intriguing because he knew the entire

Nomad tribe leaders' names, and they were the only the ones that could confine the council to a meeting. Danrak wasn't one of them, so what was this man up to, and who was he?

Barath continued reading on about this Danrak, and he found out information that he needed: that this man had been accompanied by Elmak to the desert, and once they had reached the desert they went their separate ways, Elmak going off with another rider. But every time Barath tried to find answers, he kept on finding more questions about these people that intrigued him, so he set things into motion to gain those answers.

Mardok soon realised that Barath was looking for the same people that he was, but he did not let Barath know this. Mardok soon discovered that this man didn't cover his tracks well because he eventually found out that the man he was after was in a town called Radell, and he was now travelling with an older women in her fifties. This information confirmed his suspicions that this man was defiantly a guide, so he set things into motion to see if could meet this man at the Red Lion Inn at Radell – and hopefully bribe him for the information that he wanted.

Mardok didn't know that Barath was keeping some vital information from him about these people. Barath had found out that the three companions went to Ferlinzer first, and then they split up into two groups, two people going east and this Danrak character heading to the desert. That was Barath's key; he would go east and seek out this Elmak. Without hesitation Barath abandoned his post in the army because he believed it was the right thing to do. He would go east to the village Dione where his brother Marcus lived; Marcus would know if anyone had passed through the village. If this Elmak could help him regain his honour and live proudly again, then so be it, because in the end Barath may be called a traitor – but to another person, a hero. The final say would finally come down on what happened after his defection that day.

***

Madia was on her own in the Red Lion Inn when Dany, one of her informers, told her that one of General Mardok's agents was here to talk to her. Madia allowed this agent to speak to her knowing too well that her cover as a guide had not been blown yet, and she wanted to keep it that way.

"Greetings I have come to purchase some information from you, and I will pay handsomely for it," the agent said.

"What information are you after, stranger?"

"I want to know where you took the two companions from Viscal that you guided to Ferlenzia; I am mainly interested in a man carrying a long sword."

"Ah yes, those two. Let me see, now. I think they were heading for Moradick, but I don't think that was their final destination."

"Thank you, guide. Here is twenty thousand fearings for that information, and I bid you good day."

Madia smiled at what she had done – she had just sent this man on a hopeless mission that would make him chase her phantom leads.

Mabel joined Madia at the table that was hidden in the corner of the inn. "Now that we are done with your games, Madia, where are we going?"

"We are going to Dione; it is our last destination, but before we go to Adria, we need to go my old friend Marcus's home."

"That wouldn't be the retired Colonel Marcus of the Imperial guard, would it?"

"Yes it would be. Why?"

"Oh nothing, really. I just heard about him and his mercenaries long ago." They set off without realising that they were seeking out the same person that Barath wanted to see.

CHAPTER NINE

IT HAD BEEN many months since Sammy had finally finished his training with Shakall's warriors, and he together they had created a formidable army that could probably confront Clasus's elite shock troopers. But Sammy would need more men to go up against the entire Dracell army, and when the tribe leaders arrived, Sammy planned to put that proposal forward to them, hoping that they would agree to his request.

"Danrak, my friend, I have come to know you quite well since we have met, and I do know that you are indeed a natural leader and great warrior," Takar said. "But what will you say to the council when you go before them?"

"You know, I haven't the faintest idea. I am still worried about how I am going to unite them under one banner."

Shakall patted Sammy on the back and said, "Don't worry. Lad. you will; it is your destiny."

"Thank you, Shakall, but that still won't help me with what needs to be done."

Just then a messenger arrived and said, "Come, Danrak, the council is waiting for you to speak before them."

Shakall and Sammy entered the large tent that was contained the council members. Shakall moved Sammy into the centre of the council. "Fellow council members, this is the man that I spoke of. I believe he is the one in the prophecy told all those years ago." After his introduction of Sammy to the council, Shakall took his seat within the council.

Once Shakall sat down, the oldest of the council members stood up and faced Sammy. "Greetings, Danrak, I am Zeth of the Eagle clan. Starting at my right, this is Asie of the Snake clan, Weath of the Lion clan, Traull of the Horse clan, Basier of the Raven clan, Cue of the Tiger clan, Draq of the Monkey clan, Elith of the Zebra clan, Faro of the Wolf clan, Gale of the Rabbit clan, and Haroth of the Elephant clan." There were twelve members in total, six female and six males. "We wish for you to speak before us and explain why we are here."

"Council members of the Nomad tribes, I have come here before you asking for your help! Both our people have been badly mistreated by Clasus, especially you, my friends, for the water that you need. Does this not make you angry?"

"It does, but we are no match against their army – and especially his shock troopers. We will be wiped out if we think of going against them."

"Not necessary, Zeth. If I was able to train all of the Nomad warriors, I would be able to curate any army that could go up against Clasus's shock troopers."

"Are you mad? Nothing can go up against Clasus's shock troopers!" Haroth from Elephant clan yelled.

"No, I am not mad, and I am fully aware of the consequences of what will happen if we fail – but it is a risk we must take."

"Danrak, you may have small victories against Clasus, but once Clasus sends his full wrath upon us, we won't be able to stop him."

"Have faith. You must trust me on what needs to be done."

"Very well. The council members will vote for this army that you wish to create."

"Before we vote Zeth," Haroth said, "I would like to know how Danrak is going to unite this army that we might allow him to have."

"Well, if you do give me this army," Sammy said, "you must make me the supreme commander of the army, and then I will unite my command structure as one. Once that is done, everything will fall into place."

Zeth called everyone to order and said, "Fellow council members, you have herd Danrak's words on this grand army he wishes to create. What is your vote?" One by one the council members lifted their right hands up in agreement to this army creation. "Then it is agreed. Danrak, you may have this army, and you shall be the supreme commander. Let the prophecy be filled. Farak dak teem!"

With the voting over and Danrak announced as the supreme commander, Sammy left the council members to their own agendas. "How did it go, Danrak?" Takar asked.

"Very well, my friend. I've just been made supreme commander, and my first act is to name you as my second in command. Soon we will have to combine the warriors of the Nomad tribes into a unified army."

"That is good news then."

"Yes, Haroth does concern me though, he might be trouble with our planes."

"Don't be so hard on him, Danrak. His people have had it the hardest from Clasus's wrath against us."

"Really, and how do we know that?"

"Haroth has said it to the rest of the council members; we have never doubted him before."

***

Once the council was dismissed for the day, Haroth spoke quietly to his men that he had brought with him. "Now lesion here, you lot. Danrak is no legend, and there is no legend. I will die before I will help him and that superstitious legend."

"Sir, we don't understand. You agree in the vote to help Danrak!"

"It was an elaborate ruse, you idiot. We are going give him my worst warriors. They will be leading lambs to the slaughter, and that will leave me the best warriors. My allegiance with Clasus will remain, and once we have defeated the council and their new army, I will rule the desert as king."

CHAPTER TEN

MADIA FINALLY ARRIVED at Dione with Mabel. "Welcome to Dione, the busiest town within the Empire – and it is important for its trade routes."

"Madia, why do we have to see this Marcus? Why can't we go and see Adria?"

"Have patience; we will go and see Adria soon, but we are going to need Marcus's help, so that is why we are going to him first. Come on, his house is only just down this hill." Madia lead Mabel to a small wooden house with a large, beautiful garden in front.

As they approached the house, they saw a middle-aged man in tattered clothes tending to his garden. "Hello, Madia! I thought it might be you coming down that road," the man said, and then he looked at Mabel. "Good god, Mabel! Well isn't this a surprise?"

"Yes it is, Marcus," Mabel said. "I see now that you use a trowel now instead of a sword."

"Hang on a minute you two know each other?" Madia asked.

"Yes, I knew Mabel back when she was the nurse maid to the royal family, and it seems that we have both changed since we have last seen each other."

"I am sorry to interrupt you two reminiscing about the past, but we have come here to ask for your help, Marcus, and your men as bodyguards to guard someone very special to us."

"I am retied, Madia, and you know that I want do that kind of work again; I'm no longer a mercenary or a soldier. I swore an oath that my men and I will no longer fight for the lords for their petty greeds against innocent bystanders."

"Marcus, please listen to me, we need your help. A very dear friend of mine is going to be hunted by Clasus soon, and I need someone that I can trust to protect her."

Marcus sighed and said, "You know I will do anything for you. So who is this person you want me to protect?"

Madia hugged Marcus and said, "Thank you, you won't regret this."

"I think I already have, but come anyway, let's go and sit down and discuss this more over a cup of tea, shall we?"

Marcus put his arm around Madia and walked with her and Mabel to some chairs on his patio. Madia said, "Marcus, I knew you way back when you were a soldier, and then I heard you left the Imperial guard and became a mercenary. So what happened to you? Why did you leave when you had such a high career ahead of you?"

"I left the service because I didn't believe what Clasus was doing was right anymore. I decided to become a mercenary, but in the end I just got tired of fighting for the same evil reasons as before, and I came here for some tranquillity and peace. I was fed up with looking for the heir to the throne that disappeared all those years ago."

"Marcus, my old friend, the true heir is alive, I promise you that, and has been in hiding all this years. That is the person that we want you to protect; she has finally come out in the open to claim her throne back."

"I knew it, all this years I knew she was still alive, but I just could not find her! My men are yours, Madia."

Mabel interrupted the conversation and asked, "Who is that?" She was pointing to a rider that was approaching the house.

"I don't know," Marcus said. "Wait here; I will go find out." Marcus approached the rider and then recognised the rider's face. "Hello, little brother. What brings you out here to my dwelling?"

"I have become a rogue, brother, and I am in need of your help to find a way out of what I have become," Barath said. "I have only just realised now that that you were right: Clasus is evil and needs to be stopped."

"Finally you have seen, sense, and I have some friends with me that might be what you are looking for."

"How's that?"

"You will see, Barath. My friends might have something that could eventually stop Clasus once and for all."

"I don't understand."

"Join me, brother, and we shall start a rebellion that will topple Clasus off the throne. with him gone, we shall help create a new era for the Empire."

Marcus introduced his brother to Madia and Mabel, explaining to the ladies why his brother was here. "Hello ladies I hope I am not intruding, but I want to know how my brother's men can defeat Clasus," Barath said.

"They won't be fighting the entire army; they will be just guarding someone that is a threat to Clasus," Mabel said.

"I know you from somewhere, don't I?"

"Yes you do, Barath; I was the one at the village when you took Arthur."

"Ah yes, now I remember. A bad thing that I had to do there, and I even regret doing it still."

It was starting to get dark now, so Madia and Mabel decided to leave the brothers on their own to talk things out between them. As they left, Mabel asked, "What is between you and Marcus, Madia?"

"Well we sort of have a thing between us, and I think he left the army because of me, although he denies it."

"I'm glad that young lieutenant that I once knew has finally found what he was looking for."

"Very funny, Mabel, but really I think we'll never get back together again. It was eight years later, after he had spent his time in the wilderness as a mercenary, that's when we bumped into each other again."

"You still love him. don't you. Madia?"

"Yes, that's why I told him who I really was when we meat up again; I couldn't stand lying to him anymore."

"I believe you two still love each other, but you are both too stupid to tell each other what you feel about each other."

***

Back in Marcus's house, Barath said, "Marcus, I thought you were stupid; now I know it is true. You left the service because of her."

"Yes. I love her, Barath, and I will do anything for her."

"Don't worry, I understand. I will help you in the rebellion and will fight by your side – to the end, if need be. But first. Brother. I must tell you that it was me who killed Madia's father, and I still regret it."

"Don't worry. I know what you did, but from what I hear, you spared many lives, and for that you should be proud."

CHAPTER ELEVEN

SAMMY HAD JUST finished training the Nomad army that was given to him by the council; it took longer than he had expected because he was given poorly trained warriors from the Elephant clan. Because of this he concentrated on the entire army's personal training, and eventually he united the warriors from different tribes under one banner.

Takar congratulated Sammy. "Danrak, you have done well with this army. You united them like never before, and they will fight for you."

"Don't you mean the council, Takar?"

"Forgive me, my friend, I know you wanted them be united for the council, but you haven't – they will fight for you and no one else."

"Then it looks like that I have to unite the council as well."

"I think you might have a problem there."

"Don't tell me I was right about Haroth?"

"I'm afraid so," Takar said grimly. "Our spy has just told me that Haroth has been betraying our ways for quite some time. He sits in a small fortress now with some of Clasus's elite shock troopers."

"Blast it!"

"What are we going to do Danrak?"

"I think it is time that gave our newly formed army some battle experience."

Sammy marched his army to Haroth's encampment, but he was a few miles out from the encampment when he stopped his army and confronted his newly formed command staff. "Now, my friends, we shall begin our first test on this army, and the only way is to do that is to get some battle experience with a little victory."

"What are your plans then, Danrak?" asked Haque, one of Sammy's Generals

"Before we march to Clasus, we need to secure our right flank – which is now exposed thanks to that treacherous Haroth."

"Danrak, forgive me, but even though Haroth has betrayed us, there are still rules about going up against a member of the council."

"What do you suggest then, Haque?"

"Well, I am a member of the Elephant clan, and I will challenge him for the leadership of the clan. He won't deny me this challenge, but the real problem is the shock troopers stationed there."

"Then we need to create a diversionary attack. General Sarie, I want you to lead your men to these three outposts that are near the border, and hopefully that will draw out the shock troopers to buy us the time we need to give Haque to make his challenge."

"Danrak, I trust this plan will work, because those shock troopers are the only reinforcements nearby."

"Are we set then? Good, because once General Sarie attacks with her men, the rest of the army will support Haque at the village."

General Sarie's attacks on the border outposts went according to plan, but the plan was going too well because what Danrak didn't account for was that General Sarie's army would overwhelm two of three outposts so quickly. Sammy started to worry that if the shock troops did not move out of the settlement to help the outposts, Haque wouldn't be to get in and make his challenge. However, eventually a rider was sent from the outposts to get the help from the shock troopers.

***

"Major Simons, the outposts call for aid; they are under attack by the Nomads.

"Yes, I know and I know there is also another army moving this way as well. We shall come to your aid because the main threat is at the outposts."

"You will do no such thing, Major!" barked Haroth. "You will stay here and support me against this other force."

"Don't worry, Lord Haroth, we will be back in time, and I wouldn't worry about Danrak's army because they have split up again. The main force heading this way is no match for you because you will outnumber them three to one."

***

"Danrak, I don't understand. Why split up our forces again?" Takar asked

"Well, with Sarie's forces moving faster than expected, I have to give Haroth something to make him feel safe and confident enough to move."

"Well, it seems to be working, my friend, because there they go." Takar pointed to the shock troopers leaving the fortress. Sammy moved with what forces he had left to the settlement."

Haque walked into the fortress without being checked by any of the sentries; everyone in the fortress was bowing to him because they all knew what he was going to do. They gave him respect because he was going to challenge Haroth for the leadership of the clan. "Haroth you have betrayed the Nomad ways, so I challenge you for the leadership of the clan."

"You want the leadership of the clan, do you, Haque? Then come and take it from me." Haque charged at Haroth with his spear in his hand, but before he could thrust it into Haroth, Haroth blocked it with his own spear, and with such great force behind the impact, both spears broke. Bothmen tried to go for their swords when their spears were broken, but Haroth was quicker then Haque, so Haque had to resort to hitting Haroth in the head with his shield. With Haque's quick thinking of using his shield as a weapon, he was able to go for his sword, but before he could pull it out, Haroth stabbed him in his left leg. Without a chance of bringing his sword out now, Haque decided to grab his shield by both ends and slammed it down hard upon Haroth's neck, snapping it in two and killing him instantly.

"Well done, Haque, you are now the new leader of the Elephant clan," Sammy said.

"Thank you, Danrak. So what is it you wish of my warriors?"

"I cannot command you anymore, my friend; you are a member of the council, so you must command me now because you are the closest council member to this region."

"I can't Danrak, I do not know how to!"

"Then will you take one last command from me?"

"Please, my friend."

"Haque, I can't ask anything more of you, so I ask you and your warriors to stay here and hold the outposts that we have just captured." Sammy and his troops left the building to join in the battle for the outposts.

Hours later, after the battle was finished, Sammy returned to Haque. "How did the attack go on with shock troopers General Danrak?" Haque asked.

"Very well; the second wave that I held back took them completely by surprise. What was left of them after the attack retreated to the nearest garrison."

"Congratulation, sir, you have gained your first victory."

"Thank you, Haque, but we have overstretched ourselves for the moment, so we must hold our ground and build our resources, readying for the main push – which we must do soon if I am going to keep my promise to Adria."

CHAPTER TWELVE

BACK AT MARCUS'S house, Barath told Madia the truth, why he had to kill her father. "I am glad that you have finally come out with the truth, Barath, and it saddens me that you were the one that was in charge of the platoon that horrible day. Let us hope that we shall both redeem our sins."

"Thank you for forgiving me, Madia. I think I should go and help my brother."

Barath joined his brother at the market, where Marcus could call upon his men. They both walked through the market, and at different booths Marcus put a silver token upon different people's stalls. This was Marcus's way to tell his men that he needed them. "Now we are done, my brother. Where are we going to meet your men?" Barath asked.

"The only place that is secure for us, and the place that we always meet: Sylion Mill. Let us go to the mill, and by the time we get there, Madia and Mabel should be there waiting for us with Adria."

***

It was some time later that Madia finally arrived at the old mill, and there she could clearly see that Marcus and his men had been busy building the defences around the mill. "Greetings, Madia, I see that you have an entourage with you," Barath said.

"Yes, it seems that I do, but they are needed. These two men that are with me are Doctor Lato and his apprentice, Kit. they have been looking after Adria while we have been away. Who are they, Barath?"

"Who?" Barath asked.

"Those people coming up the hill."

As Barath turned around to see what Madia was pointing at, he could see a mass of people making their way up towards the mill. "Marcus, come and have a look at this. It seems that we have visitors."

Marcus came over to see what was going on l. "Davis is that you?" he yelled.

"Yes, Marcus," a man called back. "We have heard what you've been doing within this town, and we have come to protect the true heir as well."

With the villagers joining Marcus's men, they had enough people to hold the mill against Clasus's army. "Come, Davis, we have much to talk about." Marcus led Davis into the mill and introduced him to the others that were part of the rebellion.

"Why have you come here, Davis?" Madia asked Davis.

"You will need our help. We have just heard that there are two armies heading this way: one is the Empire's and the other is the Nomad's, but I am afraid to say the Empire will arrive here first."

"Sammy!" Adria exclaimed.

"I am sorry, my lady, but I do not know this Sammy. Is he of some importance to you?"

"He is a friend of ours," Marcus explained, "and he is her lover; he will be the one that will be leading the Nomad army."

"You are mistaken, then. The man that is leading the Nomad army is called Danrak, not Sammy."

"That cannot be, it was supposed to be Sammy that leads them, not this Danrak," Madia said.

"It is, Madia!" Lato assured her.

"What are you on about, Lato?" asked Marcus. "He just told us it was a different person that leads them."

Lato ignored the comment and spoke to the ladies. "Madia, you of all people should know about secret identities. Danrak is Sammy; it his Nomad name, given to him by Shakall."

"I think we'd better get ready for Clasus's army because he certainly knows now that Adria is alive and is here, and all he needs to do is kill her to end the Dracell bloodline,"

"What about her child?"

"The child bears the same threat as Adria, – and even more of a threat when it is born."

CHAPTER THIRTEEN

CLASUS WAS PACING the floor within the war room, knowing too well what was going on within the Empire. "Right, Generals, you know what I want. I want this rebellion squashed now before it gets any more out of hand. I also want to stop the Nomad raids; is that too much to ask for?"

"My Lord, the only way we can do that is by emptying the garrisons from our northern border and marching them down to support the troops here," one general said.

"Naider, have you gone raving mad? It will take time for them to come down here, and we haven't got that time!" another said.

"I know that, Valder; that's where your men will come in; you will take them and meet up with two regular forces that are already near Dione." Naider replied.

"Very good, General Naider, a very thought-out plan. because if we can hold Dione then the capital will be secure from the Nomad invasion," Clasus said.

Just then a courier ran into the room and whispered to Valder, who spoke for all to hear. "My Lord, I have good news: I have just found out that all of the rebel leaders are gatherd up at Dione, plus one of the people that you are looking for is there."

"What! Well what are you waiting for, Valder, get a move on. I want you down there right now before the Nomad army gets there."

***

On the same day that Valder marched into Dione, Sammy also decided to take Dione as well because everyone knew if one takes Dione, it would be the key to the capital.

"Danrak?"

"What is it, Takar?"

"Your friends, they are in Dione."

"What! What are on earth are they doing there?"

"I don't know, sir, but they are safe for the time being. A friend of your sister's is protecting them; I believe he is called Marcus."

"I know this man; Madia has mentioned him to me before."

"There is one more thing, my friend. They sent a messenger to us with a message: Adria, the one that you love, is carrying your child, and it is almost time for her to give birth."

Sammy started to panic from this news. He did not know what to do and was in such a state he couldn't think straight; it was the first time in his life he felt so afraid for someone that he was immobilized for a minute. "Takar, we need to move to Dione now."

"We can't!"

"What do you mean, we can't? I want solutions, Takar, not problems."

"Danrak, my friend, please listen to me; I am trying to help you here. We are the only force that is close to Dione, and we are only eight hundred strong, a recon force. How could eight hundred men possibly go up against three thousand Imperial troops?"

"Three thousand? How on earth did they amass that many so quickly?"

"I don't know, but it seems that they have been moving a lot of troops from the north recently."

"I'm still serious, though, Takar. We need to move onto Dione no matter the cost."

"So am I, my friend. Look. I have listen to you; now will you listen to me?"

"Alright, you win, I am all ears. What is it that you wish to tell me?"

"I can do better than tell you; I will show you. Look at this map: we are at least three days from Dione, whereas Clasus's forces are only one day away – and don't forget if we get there before them we will be still be outnumbered three to one."

"The people that I care for are in that town, and I need to get them out before Clasus gets hold of them, because you know too well what he will do to them."

"My friend, I know how much you care for these people, but what you ask for is impossible."

"Nothing is impossible, Takar; you can do anything if you put your mind to it."

"I don't understand."

"Well, I think it is about time that we put my new tactic into action," Sammy said with a grin.

"You can't be serious; this cavalry is unheard of, and it hasn't even been used before."

"We have no choice. If Marcus's men can hold on for a few days, then perhaps we can do something to help them."

"People do strange things when they are in love," Takar said as he shook his head. "Very well, then. Because you have led us this far, I will follow you again, and if need be I will follow you through the gates of hell."

It took only a few hours for Takar to gather up this inexperienced cavalry. Takar didn't know how this cavalry could be used; even he didn't believe it could work, and it was never heard of before. Using men on horseback to fight as a cohesive force? But whatever way Sammy would use the cavalry, it brought another eight hundred men to the fold. So Sammy led the cavalry towards Dione, allowing Takar to pick up any other men that he could gather to help Sammy. Sammy knew this was a big gamble to take because if it didn't work, he would have a major disaster on his hands.

CHAPTER FOURTEEN

A S EVERYONE PREDICTED, it was General Valder's forces that arrived at Dione first, but he was no fool and knew about the Nomad force that was advancing towards his position very rapidly. That's what scared Valder the most:, they have moved so quickly with such a long way to travel, and now they were only six hours away from Dione. The general decided to send a small force south of Dione so he could delay this army that was moving so quickly.

***

Marcus had seen the movements of the enemy troops and thought they were going to surround him at that point, but they didn't; they just kept on going south.

"Where are they going, Marcus?" Barath asked.

"I don't know, but it may be that the Nomads are the cause of those troops going south, which means they are closer then we had thought."

But before Barath could say any more to his brother, they both heard a loud scream coming from within the mill. Marcus rushed to see what was going on, and there was Adria lying on the floor in labour. At that moment Lato rushed into the room and said, "Marcus you can't be in here; you must leave before you get in way of what needs to be done."

With Lato's help Adria pushed with all her might. "Come on, Adria, we're almost there; one more push!" And with that Adria gave birth to her daughter. Before she could relax, however, Lato said, "Hang on a minute, what's this? There is another one. Come, Adria, another push." Within a matter of seconds she gave birth to a boy. "Well done, girl, you have just given birth to two healthy twins."

"I'm so tired, Lato."

"Then rest, my dear, everything will be alright. Come here, Madia, and hold your niece." At Lato's suggestion Madia took hold of the baby girl and settled her into her arms.

Madia decided to take her niece outside and show her to Marcus. "That is the first time in a long time that I have seen joy within your eyes, Madia."

"Yes, Marcus, it has been a while, but look at this little joyful thing; isn't she lovely?"

But Marcus's eyes were looking out the window; there on the hill's rise was a black column of troops. "You must get back inside, Madia, you'll be safer in there. Tell everyone that Clasus's army has arrived."

Everybody was ready and in their positions to defend the mill, waiting for the onslaught to come. Marcus watched as the Imperial army approached. "Then it begins," he said, and with that the Imperial army attacked the defenders' lines, but one thing that Marcus could count on was that the Imperials were attacking right where he wanted them to.

"Well done, Marcus, you have forced them into a bottleneck," Davis said.

"This first wave of theirs is only a needle strike; the main strike is yet to come."

"Well it looks like they are punching throw our left flank, and hard," Barath said.

"Don't worry, brother, we will hold them."

"I hope so, because here comes the second wave now."

The second wave was a bloody and slow slogging match between both sides. The Imperials were gaining some ground, and with Barath's troops hard pressed and with little room to fight, he allowed his archers to release their fire arrows into precise locations where they had put tar down to create large explosions. This tactic had such a devastating effect upon the enemy that it gave Barath's men the room they needed to push the enemy back. With the fire arrows still raining down upon them, the Imperial troops could not attack that area while the flames still burned. "I see that your mad plan has worked, Barath," a soldier said.

"Yes, and much better than I had expected, but I am afraid that the north defences will be hard pressed now they have to face the attack."

*****

General Valder watched as this great fire burned right in front of the mill. "It seems that that they were ready for us."

"Yes, sir. They have forced our men exactly where they wanted us to be."

"Well let's change that, shall we? See if the defences on the other side of the mill are exactly the same."

The captain led a company of men to scout out the southern and eastern perimeters of the rebel defences to see what they were like. It only took a matter of moments for the captain to return to Valder. "General, I am afraid that the other sides of the mill are no good for us."

"How so, Captain?"

"Well, the south is impregnable. We cannot access it with its rocky terrain; no man can climb that."

"And the east side?"

"A marsh lies in front of it, but it may be accessible if we can find a path through it."

"Very good, Captain. I want you to lead your men through the marsh, and when you see my signal, you will attack the east wall."

Once Valder told the captain to move off with his men, he could see dust coming up from the south. Valder was out of time; the Nomads had arrived, so the only the only thing left to do was to end this war quickly – and the only way he could do that was use his shock troopers. He only hoped that the troops that he sent to challenge the Nomads could hold them off long enough to win this battle around the mill.

Valder unleashed his shock troopers straight away, knowing that he had little time to spare. The shock troopers attacked without hesitation, punching through the rebel defences. These fanatical men were so ferocious that nothing could hold them back, but thanks to Barath's quick thinking, by emptying the defenders from the other walls, they were able to hold them off for a bit longer. Everything was going well for them – until the surprise attack came from the marshes. "Marcus, there are too many of them for us hold off."

"Fall back to the entrance of the mill! That's will we make our last stand." Everybody that was left from the onslaught fell back to the entrance; there were only ten men left from the original one hundred defenders. The defenders stood there ready for the end – but it didn't come; the two sides just stood there facing each other.

"What are they waiting for Marcus?" asked Barath.

"I don't know, brother."

"They are waiting for me, Colonel Marcus!" Valder shouted as he rode into the battle.

"Valder! I should have known it would be you in charge of these men."

"You should be thanking me for sparing your life, and if it weren't for Clasus's orders wanting you all alive, you'd be dead by now."

Marcus had no choice but keep his word to Madia he would keep Adria alive – so he ordered his men to give up their arms. Valder arrested them and quickly whisked them away back to the capital. On the way back to the capital, a soldier came to Valder. "Sir, the Nomads have wiped out the force that was sent to the south, and they are coming through the gates now."

"Captain, I want you and your men to too stay here and hold the Nomads off so we can make our way back with the prisoners. Buy us that time, Captain, that is all I ask. We march to Rabien."

***

"I can't believe it, Danrak," Takar said. "Your insane plane worked. I wouldn't have believed it if I hadn't just seen the cavalry plough through the enemy column and wipe them out within seconds."

"Yes, my friend, but let us not forget why we came here in the first place." They moved on through Dione's marketplace, but as they arrived at the marked square, the Imperial soldiers attacked

58

them. The Imperials were no match against Danrak's cavalry and were easily pushed aside. "Takar take care of this will you, Takar? I am going to the mill." Sammy entered the mill and found that it was empty. He screamed in utter despair, knowing now that he was too late to help Adria.

"Danrak, we have captured someone that might be of some interest to you," Takar said as he dragged in the captain in command of the defenders at Dione.

"Well, well, look what we have here," Sammy said. "On your feet, Captain. You should face your superiors when you are spoken to."

"I will not reveal anything to you!"

"Oh don't worry, Captain, you will tell me anything that I wish to know, because do you know who I am?"

"Yes, you are the leader of the Nomad army, but that still won't make me talk."

Sammy grabbed him by the neck after that comment. "Listen here, you little worm, you will tell me what I want to know now, or I will kill you."

"General Valder has taken them to Rabien to see Clasus," the captain choked out, and when Sammy heard Clasus's name, he burst out in utter outrage and threw the captain across the room, snapping the man's neck instantly when he hit the wall.

"Now what, Danrak?" Takar asked.

"We march to the capital, and we kill Clasus."

"I might just have something for you, then. There is another force heading this way."

"How large of a force, Takar?"

"Five thousand, sir."

"Five thousand? How on earth did you mange that?"

"I didn't – it is none of our men, but it is the Imperial regular army coming over to our cause. They have just heard that Adria, the true heir, still lives."

"That's nearly the entire southern army, Takar, which means that Clasus's army is falling apart around him. We have almost done it! Clasus's power is slipping through his fingers."

CHAPTER FIFTEEN

WITHIN THE CAPITAL city's domain, Valder led his prisoners to Clasus. By now everyone in the city knew that the regular army was almost nonexistent. All Clasus had left was his faithful shock troopers to protect him.

"Welcome to the Dracell throne room, soon to be mine," Clasus said to his prisoners.

"Whatever you may think, Clasus, you are no heir, and you will never belong on that throne," Adria said.

"Well, stepsister, I know you wish to remove me from the throne, but that will depend on your Nomad friends and whether they can help you in time."

"Danrak will kill you when he gets here!"

"So that is the name of the Nomad general that has decimated my army, and now he is on his way here for you, stepsister." But little did he know that Sammy was already outside the capital trying to break down the citadel gates.

Sammy finally broke through the citadel gates and made his way through the capital's defences. It was hard going because although the Imperial troops were now fighting on Sammy's side, the shock troopers were making them fight for every bit of ground. Both sides lost many men, but the Imperial regular army fought with such courage and determination that it was enough to push back the shock troopers towards the palace.

While the Imperials were fighting the shock trooper's, Sammy moved off with his faithful soldiers on foot through some back alleyways, away from the fighting. Thanks to Danrak the cavalry was trained to fight both ways, on foot and on horseback, which made them a more effective force that way. They were moving quickly through the streets towards the grand hall, and they almost got to the main building when all of a sudden fighting broke out right in front of them, blocking their path. They had no option but to fight through the mass of people and see if they could get into the great hall.

Some of his men made it through the fighting into the great hall, and they made good progress passing through the corridors very quickly. "It's too quiet, Danrak. I don't like it," Takar said nervously.

"Indeed, it seems that Clasus has got something planed for us." Immediately after Sammy said those words, the shock troopers sprung their trap. They stepped out in front of Sammy's men, taking them completely by surprise – and these shock troopers were different from the usual ones: they were dressed in a full suit of armour from head to toe, and they held a six-foot kite shield and a rapier sword.

The sergeant of the shock troopers wore an orange patch on his right shoulder that identified his rank. He stepped forward and addressed Sammy and his men. "Soldiers of the Nomad tribes, you have fought gallantly to get this far, but you will go no further. Surrender your arms now, and your lives shall be spared."

"What shall we do, Danrak?"

"Do exactly what he says, Takar; we shall surrender to them."

"You can't be serous!"

"Takar, trust me in this; I know what I am doing." Danrak gave Takar a wink, indicating that he had something planed for them, and then he spoke to the enemy. "Very well, Sergeant, we shall surrender, but under your Imperial laws of justice: that our arms shall not be taken until the emperor or empress deems otherwise."

The sergeant looked as if he couldn't believe what he was hearing – the Imperial laws were being quoted by a Nomad. The sergeant regained his composure from this shock, gathered up his prisoners, and took them to Clasus.

As Sammy entered the great hall, there upon the dais was Clasus staring down upon them. "Ah, at last the mighty Danrak has been brought before me. Look how far you have fallen, desert rat."

"This rat has not fallen yet, Clasus."

"Yes, I can see the arrogance within those eyes of yours. I expect you to call me out in combat because according to your rules, that is the only way you can gain leadership."

"No, I haven't come to challenge you by the Nomad ways! But I have come here to fight you for my family's honour."

"You have no honour here, desert rat. You're not even an Imperial citizen."

"That is where you are wrong, Clasus. I am an Imperial citizen, so I have every right to gain my family honour back."

"How can this be?"

"I am Sammy, nephew of Arthur, and I am the last of the Chosen Ones."

Clasus's face drained of colour once he had heard this; it seemed that his most dreaded dream had come true. He quickly regained his composure and said, "So the pieces are set now; the last traitor to the Empire has come before me. You have betrayed your emperor for the last time, desert rat."

"I am not the traitor here, Clasus – you are."

"How dare you speak to your emperor that way!"

Adria spoke up from the side of the room. "Don't make yourself comfortable, Clasus, because you are not the true heir to the throne. I am."

"You lie, stepsister!"

"Let her speak," said General Naider. "I am intrigued by what she has to say."

"Very well, Naider, I will grant you this wish," Clasus said. "Because you know I have the right to sit upon the Imperial throne, and she does not."

"I am the only one here of Dracell blood, Clasus," Adria said.

"Ridiculous! There is no other heir."

"General Naider, look at this ring," Adria continued. "It shows that I speak the truth: I am the true heir, the daughter of Frances II and of his second wife. Clasus is nothing but an impostor that wishes he was the emperor."

"I don't believe it," Naider said. "In all my years as the supreme commander, I have only served two emperors in my lifetime. Forgive me, my lady, I did not know. I serve the Empire, not the person that sits upon the throne." With that Naider and most of the generals went over to Adria and swore their allegiance to her.

Clasus was angry now with everything going wrong for him, so he charged at her with his sword, but before he could strike Sammy intervened by blocking Clasus with his long sword, and as he did so the blade turned gold and shattered Clasus's sword instantly.

"Well done, I salute you, desert rat," Clasus spat. "I believe this leaves only one thing left for us to do." Clasus prepared to fight hand to hand.

Sammy passed his sword to Takar and then faced Clasus in the Chosen One fighting stance. Clasus charged at Sammy, and the both of them collided with each other in battle. While they were fighting between each other, the Nomad soldiers that came with Sammy were secretly passing weapons to Marcus's mercenaries under the shock troopers' noses. Once they were fully armed, they attacked their captors, and the guards were caught off guard because they were keeping an eye on Clasus's fight instead of the prisoners, but they soon realised what was going on and fought back.

Adria didn't care what was going on around her; all she cared about was Sammy. She was concerned because it looked like that he was losing to Clasus's superior strength. Adria grabbed Takar's arm when Clasus knocked Sammy on his back. Takar knew what was going on with this fight, and with his honour bound to his friend, he would never leave Adria's side. "It's okay dear, it's alright. Clasus just got a lucky punch, that's all." Before he could say more, Sammy did a back flip and started to attack Clasus in a different technique that the emperor hadn't seen before. Adria soon realised now that she was seeing the vision that she had the night she slept with Sammy in Ferlenzer.

Clasus couldn't defend against Danrak's different fighting style. Sammy's attack was endless and without hesitation. He used combinations of kicks and punches against Clasus, and then he brought a roundhouse kick against Clasus's head breaking his neck and ending his life. Everyone was still as stone when they saw Clasus drop to the floor dead. Adria ran over to Sammy once he had his victory, ready to embrace him in her arms, but before she could reach him Sammy collapsed to his knees from exhaustion. When she finally reached him a group of Nomads followed her and surrounded the couple in a protective bubble.

"Sammy, my love, are you all right?"

"Yes, Adria, I am fine, just a little tired from the fight, that's all. It looks like we are not finished here, Takar."

"Yes," Takar said, "but it seems that they are being taken care of." While the soldiers were attending to Sammy, a mob of the citizens broke in and joined the fight against the shock troopers.

Adria finally hugged Sammy, and he took her into his arms. "Oh. Sammy. I missed you so much!?"

"I have missed you also. But come, Adria, it's time we did what we came here to do." With that Sammy got up back on his feet, took Adria's hand, and escorted her to the throne. She sat down upon the throne, and Sammy yelled, "Hail Adria, Empress of the Dracell Empire!" when Sammy shouting out his acknowledgement for Adria, everyone got down onto their knees for their true leader.

One man got up off his knee and spoke to Adria. "My lady, we are thankful that you are now fully restored to the throne, and we hope that you will bring the peace and prosperity to the Empire that we have so wanted while under Clasus's rule."

"Thank you very much, citizen. You shall all get the good fortune that you have asked for. Tomorrow you shall all see me be crowned as your empress."

Once everyone was happy with Adria's words, they all left, taking the dead with them. Mabel and Madia walked over to Sammy and passed him his two children. "Say hello to your children, Sammy." Mabel said.

"Congratulations, brother, you are now a father," said Madia.

"What are their names?" Sammy asked Adria.

"I haven't named them yet; I was waiting for you to help me."

"You know, Adria, it will be weird when they grow up. Our son is going to be emperor, and our daughter will sit at the Nomad council. So if our daughter is going to sit at the Nomad council, she should have a Nomad name. I like the name Dowine, "queen of the desert," but I don't know what to call our son."

"I think we should call him after his father."

"Okay, we'll call him Sammy. But I don't like two people within the family being called by same name, so from now on I shall be called only by my Nomad name."

On the day of Adria's coronation, everybody came to see her be crowned, and though the grand hall was packed, there were others still piling in trying to get a glimpse of their empress. Once she had acknowledged the lords and the Nomad council that came to watch, she sat down upon the dais, and the high priest crowned her as Adria the First. "Let everyone here see their empress that will rule over us," the priest announced.

"Citizens of this great nation," Adria said, "I present to you my children: my heir, Sammy, and his twin sister, Dowine, who will be the next leader of Bear clan and will have a seat upon the No-mad council. This will be bond that we shall have with our Nomad friends."

"Adria," the Nomad spokesman said, "We accept this bond of friendship between the Dracell clan. But we also wish that Danrak would come back with us to the desert and help us rebuild our na-tion."

Adria looked to Sammy to see what he would say but she al-ready knew: he would go back and help the Nomads unite as one. It was the price that he had to pay to gain their help for Adria.

Danrak said, "Shakall, I shall remain as the Nomads supreme commander until I have united the tribes as I have promised."

Throughout the day, other people were given honours from Adria for their service to the Empire for helping her. When the day was nearly over, Adria had a private meeting with her closest friends and allies. Within her private meeting, she gave Barath the position of intelligence officer. She tried to give Marcus the position of su-preme commander, but he declined the position and instead decided to settle down with Madia at his home in Dione. Mabel was happy that she had seen the children that she had helped raise reach the positions they were in now; she died a year later, happy that the Em-pire became a peaceful nation once again. Six years later, Sammy finally returned to Adria, passing on his Nomad command to his good friend, Takar.

In the many years that Adria would rule with Sammy by her side, she ruled in peace and harmony. All the people would say that Adria ruled by the kindness of her heart, and that Danrak would keep the laws just and fair for all the people within the Empire.